To those
with the wisdom to refer to this as
the "Scottish" play.

Sixty-Minute Shakespeare
MACBETH

by
Cass Foster

First Edition 1990.
Second Edition 1997.Third Edition 1998.Fourth Edition 2000.
All rights reserved. Printed in the United States of America.

Library of Congress Cataloging-in-Publication Data

Foster, Cass, 1948—
   The Sixty-Minute Shakespeare--[abridged] / Cass Foster.--1st ed.
     p. Cm. —(Classics for all ages)
   Summary: An abridged version of Shakespeare's tragedy about
witches, prophesies, blind ambition, murder and corruption.

ISBN: 1-877749-41-9

1. Macbeth, King of Scotland. 11th cent. —Juvenile drama.
2. Middle Ages—Juvenile drama. 3. Children's plays, English
[1. Macbeth, King of Scotland, 11th cent.—Drama. 2. Plays.].
I. Shakespeare, William. 1564-1616 Macbeth. II. Title. III. Series.
PR2831.A25 1997
822.3'3—dc21   97-28919
                                                          CIP
                                                           AC

Cover Design by Barbara Kordesh
Paul M. Howey, Copy Editor

Five Star Publications, Incorporated
P.O. Box 6698
Chandler, AZ 85246-6698
websiter: www.fivestarsupport.com
e-mail: info@fivestarsupport.com

Five Star Publications, Incorporated

Where education comes naturally.

The Sixty-Minute Shakespeare:

Macbeth

by
Cass Foster

from

The Tragedy of Macbeth

by
William Shakespeare

Five Star Publications, Incorporated ★ Chandler, AZ

Welcome to *The Sixty-Minute Shakespeare*

Thanks to the progressive thinking of so many curriculum developers, Language Arts people and the splendid film work being done by directors such as Kenneth Branagh and Franco Zeffirelli, there has been a phenomenal growth in interest in Shakespeare.

No playwright, past or present, approaches the brilliance and magnitude of William Shakespeare. What other individual has even come close to understanding and then dramatizing the human condition? Just for the fun of it, I am listing (following these introductory remarks) a sample of themes and images so richly developed in the canon of his plays.

Shakespeare's characters are so well-rounded and beautifully constructed that it is common to see them as actual historical figures. When someone mentions Hamlet, Iago, Ophelia, or Puck, we immediately experience images and emotions that come from memories of people we know. We may feel compassion, frustration, sorrow, or pleasure.

As one of the wealthiest people of his times, Shakespeare earned his living as a playwright, theatre manager, actor, and shareholder in the Globe Theatre. He worked tirelessly to entertain (Theatres presented a new play every day and the average new play had a total of only ten performances over an entire season.) He rebelled against the contemporary theatrical standards (the neo-classical principles that limited dramatic structure throughout France and Italy), he took plots from other published works (making them uniquely his own), and he created a spectacle (without the use of elaborate scenery) to captivate audiences of all social levels.

Imagine the challenge in quieting a crowd of three thousand in a theatre where vendors sell wine, beer, ale, nuts, and cards; where there is no intermission; where birds fly overhead; and where audience members stand near performers. Such was the settings which Shakespeare's plays were originally staged.

The world's most familiar and successful wordsmith used language to skillfully create images, plot, and a sense of music and rhythm. The purpose behind this series is to reduce (not contemporize) the language. The unabridged Shakespeare simply isn't practical in all situations. Not all educators or directors have the luxury of time to explore the entire text. This is not intended to be a substitute for a thorough study of Shakespeare. It is merely a stepping stone.

I challenge each of you to go beyond the *Sixty-Minute* versions. Use the comfort, appreciation, and self-confidence you will gain to go further. Be proud of the insights and knowledge you acquire but do not be satisfied. The more you read, the more you gain.

I would love to know what you like about the design of this series and what we might do to improve it. I encourage our readers outside the United States to let me know how well this series works for you. It would also help to know what other Shakespearean plays you would like in the *Sixty-Minute* format. **Please e-mail me at *casspeare@usa.net*.**

May each of you be blessed with an abundance of good health and happiness. I thank you for your interest in our work and hope your are pleased with what we have done.

May the Verse Be With You!

iv

A couple of staging considerations.

<u>Scenery</u>

There are two excellent reasons theatres rarely use much scenery when staging Shakespeare. The first is related to the number of changes required. If we have to wait every five to ten minutes to watch scenery struck and set up, we end up watching a play about moving lumber. The second reason is that we lose sight of what the play is about. Audiences need a couple minutes to adjust to the new scenic look of a dazzling waterfall and lush forest. By the time they take it all in and start paying attention to what the actors are saying, it is time to set up the next scene and the audience is lost.

Location is normally established through dialogue and the use of a few simple props: a throne-like chair for the king's court, a long table with benches for an inn, or a bed for the queen's bed chamber. The key is to keep it simple.

<u>Pacing</u>

You will want to keep things moving all the time. That doesn't mean actors should talk and move quickly; it simply means one scene should flow smoothly to the next without delay or interruption.

As scene one ends, the actors pick up their props and walk off. Actors for scene two enter from a different direction with their props and begin dialogue as soon as they enter the acting area, putting their props in place as they speak. Yes, we will still have view of the actors in the first scene, but your audience will gladly accept this convention if it means taking fifteen minutes off performance time.

Images and themes to look for in the various plays

Mistaken identity

Insanity

Religious persecution

The supernatural

Loneliness or isolation

Conspiracy

Hypocrisy

Pride

Violence

Rebellion

Seduction

Loyalty

Marriage

Irresponsible power

Real or pretended madness

Tyranny

Spying

Play-acting

Heavenly retribution

Witchcraft

Self-destruction

Animals

Reality vs. illusion

Characters reforming

Freedom

Fertility

Sexual misadventure

Corrupt society

Multiple meanings of words

Impetuous love

Human frailty

Charity

Wisdom of fools

Greed and corruption

The elements

Darkness and light

Anti-Semitism

Revenge

Abandonment

Honor

Bravery

Savagery

Disease or physical decay

War

False accusations

Destiny or fate

Ambition

Foils or opposites

Paranoia

Justice

Forgiveness

Mortality

Black or white magic

Nature

Astrological influence

Old age

Usurping of power

Suppression

Melancholy

Love and/or friendship

Thought vs. action

Role of women

Preparing for leadership

Betrayal

The Complete Works of William Shakespeare

1589 - 1591	Henry VI, Part 1, 2 and 3
1592 - 1593	Richard III
1593 - 1594	Titus Andronicus
1592 - 1594	Comedy of Errors
1593 - 1594	Taming of the Shrew
1594	The Two Gentlemen of Verona
1594 - 1595	Love's Labour's Lost
1594 - 1596	King John
1595	Richard II
1595 - 1596	A Midsummer Night's Dream
1595 - 1596	Romeo and Juliet
1596 - 1597	The Merchant of Venice
1597	The Merry Wives of Windsor
1597 - 1598	Henry IV, Part 1 and 2
1598 - 1599	Much Ado About Nothing
1599	Henry V
1599	Julius Caesar
1599	As You Like It
1600 - 1601	Hamlet
1601 - 1602	Twelfth Night
1601 - 1602	Troilus and Cressida
1602 - 1603	All's Well That Ends Well
1604	Measure for Measure
1604	Othello
1605	The Tragedy of King Lear
1606	Macbeth
1606 - 1607	Antony and Cleopatra
1607 - 1608	Timon of Athens
1607 - 1608	Pericles, Prince of Tyre
1607 - 1608	Coriolanus
1609 - 1610	Cymbeline
1609 - 1610	The Winter's Tale
1611	The Tempest
1612 - 1613	Henry VIII
1613	Two Noble Kinsmen (Authorship in question.)

April 23, 1564 - April 23, 1616

"If we wish to know the force of human genius, we should read Shakespeare. If we wish to see the insignificance of human learning, we may study his commentators."

William Hazlitt (1778-1830), English Essayist. "On the Ignorance of the Learned," in *Edinburgh Magazine* (July, 1818).

Common Quotes from the Bard.

Romeo and Juliet

> Parting is such sweet sorrow.
> A plague o' both your houses.
> O Romeo, Romeo! Wherefore art thou Romeo?

A Midsummer Night's Dream

> Lord, what fools these mortals be.
> The course of true love never did run smooth.
> To say the truth, reason and love keep little company
> together now-a-days.

As You Like It

> All that glisters is not gold.
> Love is blind.
> All the world's a stage
> And all the men and women merely players.
> For ever and a day.

Twelfth Night

> Some are born great, some achieve greatness, and some have
> greatness thrust upon them.
> Out of the jaws of death.
> O, had I but followed the arts!
> Many a good hanging prevents a bad marriage.

Henry IV, Part 1

> The better part of valour is discretion.
> To give the devil his due.
> He hath eaten me out of house and home.

King Lear
> The Prince of Darkness is a gentleman.

Henry VI, Part 2

> Let's kill all the lawyers.

The Merry Wives of Windsor

> Better three hours too soon than a minute too late.

Common Quotes from the Bard.

Macbeth

> Out, damned spot. Out, I say!
> Screw your courage to the sticking place.

Hamlet

> Something is rotten in the state of Denmark.
> To be or not to be. That is the question.
> The lady doth protest too much, methinks.
> Good night, sweet prince, And flights of angels
>   sing thee to thy rest!

The Merchant of Venice

> The devil can cite scriptures for his purpose.

Pericles

> Few love to hear the sins they love to act.

Richard III

> Now is the winter of our discontent.
> Off with his head!
> A horse! A horse! My kingdom for a horse.

Julius Caesar

> Beware the ides of March.
> Friends, Romans, countrymen, lend me your ears.
> It was Greek to me.

Much Ado About Nothing

> The world must be peopled. When I said I would die a
>   bachelor, I did not think I should live till I were
>   married.

Measure for Measure

> The miserable have no other medicine but only hope.

Troilus and Cressida

> To fear the worst oft cures the worse.

The Comedy of Errors

> Unquiet meals make ill digestions.

Cast of characters

Duncan, King of Scotland
Malcolm, his son
Donalbain, his son
Macbeth, general in the King's army
Banquo, general in the King's army

Noblemen of Scotland:

Macduff	*Menteth*
Lennox	*Angus*
Ross	*Cathness*

Fleance, son of Banquo
Siward, Earl of Northumberland, general of the English forces
Young Siward, his son
Seyton, an officer attending on Macbeth
Boy, son to Macduff

English Doctor	*Porter*
Scots Doctor	*Three Murderers*
Captain	

Lady Macbeth
Lady Macduff
Gentlewomen attending on Lady Macbeth

Three Witches, the Weird Sisters
Three Apparitions
Lords, Gentlemen, Officers, Soldiers, Attendants and Messengers.

Place
Scotland and England

Act I, Scene 1 is cut.

Act I, Scene 2.

A camp in Scotland.

Alarum within°. *Enter King [Duncan], Malcolm, Donalbain, Lennox, with Attendants, meeting the bleeding Captain.*

King. What bloody man is that?

Malcolm.   This is the Sergeant°
   Who like a good and hardy soldier fought
   'Gainst my captivity. Hail, brave friend!
   Say to the king the knowledge of the broil°
   As thou didst leave it.

Captain. Brave Macbeth—well he deserves that name—
   Disdaining fortune, with his brandished steel,
   Which smoked with bloody execution,
   Like valor's minion° carved out his passage
   Till he faced the slave, Macdonwald;
   Which never shook hands, nor bade farewell to him,
   Till he unseamed him from the nave to th' chops°,
   And fixed his head upon our battlements.

King. O valiant cousin°! Worthy gentleman!

Captain. Mark, King of Scotland, mark:
   No sooner justice had, with valor armed,
   Compelled these skipping kerns to trust their heels

Alarum within: **trumpet calls offstage.** *Sergeant:* officer. *Broil:* battle. *Minion:* favorite. *Chops:* jaws. *Cousin:* kinsmen. (Duncan and Macbeth were grandsons of King Malcolm).

1

[Captain.] But the Norweyan lord, surveying vantage°,
  With furbished arms and new supplies of men,
  Began a fresh assault.

King.   Dismayed not this
  Our captains, Macbeth and Banquo?

Captain. Yes; as sparrows eagles, or the hare the lion.
  If I say sooth°, I must report they were
  As cannons overcharged with double cracks°;
  But I am faint; my gashes cry for help.

King. So well thy words become thee as thy wounds;
  They smack of honor both. Go get him surgeons.

Exit Captain and Attendant as Ross and Angus enter.

King. Who comes here?

Malcolm.   The worthy Thane° of Ross.

Ross. G-d° save the king!

King. Whence cam'st thou worthy Thane?

Ross.   From Fife, great King;
  Where the Norweyan banners flout the sky
  And fan our people cold.

Surveying vantage: seeing an opportunity. *Sooth*: truth. *Cracks*: explosives. *Thane*: title of nobility. *G-d:* According to the editor's religious convictions, to write out the name of the Supreme Being in full turns the text into a sacred scripture. Out of respect for his beliefs, we will hyphenate all usage.

2

Ross: Norway°himself, with terrible numbers,
    Assisted by that most disloyal traitor
    The Thane of Cawdor, began a dismal° conflict;
    Till that Bellona's bridegroom, lapped in proof°,
    Confronted him with self-comparisons°,
    Point against point, rebellious arm 'gainst arm,
    Curbing his lavish° spirit: and, to conclude,
    The victory fell on us.

King.   Great happiness!

Ross. Norway's king craves composition°;
    Nor would he deign him burial of his men
    Till he disbursèd, at Saint Colme's Inch°,
    Ten thousand dollars° to our general use.

King. No more that Thane of Cawdor shall deceive
    Our bosom interest°: go pronounce his present° death,
    And with his former title greet Macbeth.

Ross. I'll see it done.

King. What he hath lost, noble Macbeth hath won.

All exit.

Norway: King of Norway. *Dismal:* threatening. *Lapped in proof:* clad in armor.
Self-comparison: equally valiant deeds. *Lavish:* wild. *Composition:* terms of peace.
Saint Colme's Inch: Incholm, a small island. *Dollars:* Spanish and Dutch currency.
Bosom interest: trusting heart. *Present:* immediate.

Act I, Scene 3.
A heath.

Thunder. Enter the three Witches.

First Witch. Where hast thou been, sister?

Second Witch. Killing swine.

First Witch. Thou art kind.

Drum offstage.

Third Witch. A drum, a drum!
    Macbeth doth come.

All. The weird° sisters, hand in hand,
    Posters of° the sea and land,
    Thus do go about, about;
    Thrice to thine, and thrice to mine,
    And thrice again, to make up nine.
    Peace! The charm's wound up°.

Enter Macbeth and Banquo.

Macbeth. So foul and fair a day I have not seen.

Banquo.   What are these
    So withered, and so wild in their attire,
    That look not like th' inhabitants o' th' earth,
    And yet are on 't? You should be women,

Weird: destiny-driven. *Posters of*: swift travelers over. *Wound up: i.e.* ready for action.

Banquo. And yet your beards forbid me to interpret
   That you are so.

Macbeth.   Speak, if you can: what are you?

First Witch. All hail, Macbeth! Hail to thee, Thane of Glamis!

Second Witch. All hail, Macbeth! Hail to thee, Thane of
   Cawdor!

Third Witch. All hail, Macbeth, that shalt be King hereafter!

First Witch. Hail!

Second Witch. Hail!

Third Witch. Hail!

First Witch. Lesser than Macbeth, and greater.

Second Witch. Not so happy°, yet much happier.

Third Witch. Thou shalt get° kings, though thou be none.

   So all hail, Macbeth and Banquo!

First Witch. Banquo and Macbeth, all hail!

Macbeth. Stay, you imperfect° speakers, tell me more:
   By Sinel's° death I know I am Thane of Glamis;
   But how of Cawdor? The Thane of Cawdor lives.
   Say from whence you owe° this strange intelligence°?
   Speak, I charge you. *[Witches vanish]*

Happy: fortunate. *Get*: beget. *Imperfect*: incomplete. *Sinel*: Macbeth's father.
Owe: have. *Intelligence*: information.

[Macbeth.]   Would they have stayed!

Banquo. Were such things here as we do speak about?
     Or have we eaten on the insane° root
     That takes the reason prisoner? You shall be King.

Macbeth. And Thane of Cawdor too. Went it not so?

Banquo. To th' selfsame tune and words. Who's there?

Enter Ross and Angus.

Ross. The King hath happily received, Macbeth,
     The news of thy success; and when he reads°
     Thy personal venture in the rebels' fight,
     His wonders and his praises do contend
     Which should be thine or his°.

Angus.   We are sent
     To give thee, from our royal master, thanks;
     Only to herald thee into his sight, not pay thee.

Ross. And for an earnest° of a greater honor,
     He bade me, from him, call thee Thane of Cawdor;
     In which addition°, hail, most worthy Thane!
     For it is thine.

Banquo.   What, can the devil speak true?

Macbeth. The Thane of Cawdor lives: why do you dress me
     In borrowed robes?

Insane: insanity causing.   *Reads:* considers.   *His...his:* Duncan is speechless. He
doesn't know if he should speak of astonishment or admiration.   *Earnest:* pledge.
Addition: title.

6

Angus.   Who was the thane lives yet,
But treasons capital, confessed and proved,
Have overthrown him.

Macbeth. [Aside] Glamis, and Thane of Cawdor:
The greatest is behind°. *[To Ross and Angus]* Thanks
for your pains.

Banquo leads Ross and Angus off to the side.

Macbeth. [Aside] This supernatural soliciting°
Cannot be ill, cannot be good. If ill,
Why hath it given me earnest of success,
Commencing in a truth? I am Thane of Cawdor:
If good, why do I yield to that suggestion
Whose horrid image doth unfix my hair
And make my seated° heart knock at my ribs,
Against the use of nature°?

Banquo. Look, how our partner's rapt.
Worthy Macbeth, let us toward the King.

Macbeth. [Aside to Banquo] Think upon what hath
chanced, and at more time,
The interim having weighed it°, let us speak
Our free hearts° each to other.

Banquo.   Very gladly.

Macbeth. Till then, enough...Come, friends. *[They all exit]*

Behind: to come. *Soliciting*: inviting. *Seated*: fixed. *Against... of nature*: unlike my
natural way. *The interims...weighed it*: *i.e.* when we have time to think this through.
Free hearts: our minds freely.

Act I, Scene 4.

Forres. The palace.

*Flourish °. Enter King [Duncan], Lennox, Malcolm,
Donalbain, and Attendants.*

King. Is execution done on Cawdor? Are not
   Those in commission° yet returned?

Malcolm.   My liege,
   They are not yet come back. But I have spoke
   With one that saw him die, who did report
   That very frankly he confessed his treasons,
   Implored your Highness' pardon and set forth
   A deep repentance.

King. He was a gentleman on whom I built
   an absolute trust.

Enter Macbeth, Banquo, Ross and Angus.

Malcolm.   O worthiest cousin!
   The sin of my ingratitude even now
   Was heavy on me: thou art so far before,
   That swiftest wing of recompense is slow
   To overtake thee.

Macbeth. The service and the loyalty I owe,
   In doing it, pays itself°. Our duties
   Are to your throne and state children and servants.

King.   Welcome hither.

Flourish: fanfare offstage. *In commission:* chosen to represent me at the execution.
Pays itself: is its own reward.

King. I have begun to plant thee, and will labor
    To make thee full of growing. Noble Banquo,
    That hast no less deserved, nor must be known
    No less to have done so, let me enfold thee
    And hold thee to my heart.

Banquo. There if I grow, the harvest is your own.

King.   My plenteous joys,
    Wanton° in fullness, seek to hide themselves
    In drops of sorrow. Sons, kinsmen, thanes,
    And you whose places are the nearest, know,
    We will establish our estate° upon
    Our eldest, Malcolm, whom we name hereafter
    The Prince of Cumberland. From hence to Inverness,
    And bind us further to you.

Macbeth. The rest is labor, which is not used for you°.
    I'll be myself the harbinger° and make joyful
    The hearing of my wife with your approach;
    So, humbly take my leave.

King.   My worthy Cawdor!

Macbeth. [Aside] The Prince of Cumberland! That is a step
    On which I must fall down, or else o'erleap,
    For in my way it lies. *[Macbeth exits.]*

King. It is a banquet to me. Let's after him,
Whose care is gone before to bid us welcome. *[They exit]*

Wanton: unrestrained. *Establish our estate*: settle the question of succession. *The rest is labor... you*: i.e. pleasure not spend in your service is undesirable. *Harbinger:* one sent ahead to arrange lodging.

Act I, Scene 5.
Inverness. Macbeth's castle.

Enter Lady Macbeth, Macbeth's wife, alone, with a letter.

Lady M. [Reads] "They met me in the day of success; and I
have learned by the perfect'st report they have more in
them than mortal knowledge. When I burned in desire to
question them further, they made themselves air, into which
they vanished. Whiles I stood rapt in the wonder of it, came
missives° from the King, who all-hailed me 'Thane of
Cawdor'; by which title, before, these weird sisters saluted
me, and referred me to the coming on of time, with 'Hail,
King that shalt be!' This have I thought good to deliver
thee°, my dearest partner of greatness, that thou mightst
not lose the dues of rejoicing, by being ignorant of what
greatness is promised thee. Lay it to thy heart, and farewell."

Glamis thou art, and Cawdor, and shalt be
What thou art promised. Yet do I fear thy nature;
It is too full o' th' milk of human kindness°
To catch the nearest way. Thou wouldst be great,
Art not without ambition, but without
The illness° should attend it...Hie thee hither,
That I may pour my spirits in thine ear,
And chastise with the valor of my tongue
All that impedes thee from the golden round°
Which fate and metaphysical° aid doth seem
To have thee crowned withal°.

Missives: messengers. *Deliver thee:* report to you. *Milk of human kindness:*
kindheartedness. *Illness:* wickedness. *Round:* crown. *Metaphysical:* supernatural.
Withal: with.

Enter Messenger.

Lady M. What is your tidings?

Messenger. The King comes here tonight.

Lady M.   Thou'rt mad to say it!
Is not thy master with him, who, were't so,
Would have informed for preparation?

Messenger. So please you, it is true. Our thane is coming.
One of my fellows had the speed of him°,
Who, almost dead for breath, had scarcely more
Than would make up his message.

Lady M.   Give him tending;
He brings great news.

Exit Messenger.

Lady M.   Come, you spirits
That tend on mortal° thoughts, unsex me here,
And fill me, from the crown to the toe, top-full
Of direst cruelty! Make thick my blood.
Come to my woman's breasts,
And take my milk for° gall. Come, thick night,
And pall thee° in the dunnest° smoke of hell,
That my keen knife see not the wound it makes,
Nor heaven peep through the blanket of the dark,
To cry "Hold, hold!"

Speed of him: outdistanced him.   *Mortal:* deadly.   *For:* in exchange for.   *Pall thee:*
wrap yourself.   *Dunnest:* darkest.

11

Enter Macbeth.

Lady M.   Great Glamis! Worthy Cawdor!
  Greater than both, by the all-hail hereafter!
  Thy letters have transported me beyond
  This ignorant° present, and I feel now
  The future in the instant°.

Macbeth. My dearest love, Duncan comes here tonight.

Lady M.   And when goes hence?

Macbeth. Tomorrow, as he proposes.

Lady M. O, never shall sun that morrow see!
  Your face, my Thane, is as a book where men
  May read strange matters. Look like th' innocent flower,
  But be the serpent under't. You shall put
  This night's great business into my dispatch°.

Macbeth. We will speak further.

Lady M.   Only look up clear°.
  To alter favor ever is to fear°. Leave all the rest to me.

They exit.

Ignorant: unknowing of the future. *Instant:* present. *Dispatch:* management. *Look up clear:* appear undisturbed. *To alter...fear:* to look disturbed can be dangerous.

Please note:
Not everyone realizes it is not only illegal to photocopy copyrighted material but by photocopying (and reducing sales) small publishing houses like ours will not be able to generate sufficient resources to create additional works. We appreciate your understanding and assistance.

Act I, Scene 6.
Inverness. Before Macbeth's castle.

*Hautboys ° and torches. Enter King [Duncan], Malcolm,
Donalbain, Banquo, Lennox, Macduff, Ross, Angus, and
Attendants.*

King. This castle has a pleasant seat°.

Banquo. This guest of summer, the temple-haunting marlet°,
  Where they most breed and haunt, I have observed
  The air is delicate.

Enter Lady Macbeth.

King.   See, see, our honored hostess!
  The love that follows us sometime is our trouble,
  Which still we thank as love°. Herein I teach you
  How you shall bid G-d 'ield° us for your pains
  And thank us for your trouble.

Lady M.   All our service
  In every point twice done, and then done double,
  Were poor and single business° to contend
  Against those honors deep and broad wherewith
  Your majesty loads our house: for those of old,
  and the late dignities heaped up to them,
  We rest your ermits°.

Hautboys: oboes. *Seat*: site. *Temple-haunting marlet*: bird (martin) that builds its
next in churches. *The love that follows...as love*: even if your offerings inconvenience
me, I still appreciate your love. *'ield*: reward. *Single business*: feeble service. *Rest
your ermites*: we will always pray for you.

13

King.   Where's the Thane of Cawdor?
   We coursed° him at the heels, but he rides well.
   Fair and noble hostess, we are your guest tonight.

Lady M. Your servants ever.

King.   Give me your hand.
   Conduct me to mine host: we love him highly,
   And shall continue our graces toward him.

They exit.

Act I, Scene 7.
Macbeth's castle.

Enter Macbeth.

Macbeth. If it were done when 'tis done, then 'twere well
   It were done quickly. If th' assassination
   Could trammel up° the consequence, and catch,
   With his surcease°, success°; that but this blow
   Might be the be-all and the end-all. But in these cases
   We still° have judgement° here; that we but teach
   Bloody instructions, which, being taught, return
   To plague th' inventor...I have no spur
   To prick the sides of my intent, but only
   Vaulting ambition, which o'erleaps itself
   And falls on th' other-

Enter Lady Macbeth.

Coursed: pursued.   *Trammel up*: entangle as in a net.   *His surcease*: Duncan's death.
Success: what follows.   *Still*: always.   *Have judgement*: are punished.

14

[Macbeth.]   How now! What news?

Lady M. Why have you left the chamber?

Macbeth. Hath he asked for me?

Lady M. Know you not he has? Was the hope drunk
      Wherein you dressed yourself? Hath it slept since?
      Art thou afeared to be the same in thine
      Own act and valor as thou art in desire?

Macbeth.   Prithee, peace!
      I dare do all that may become a man;
      Who dares do more is none.

Lady M.   What beast was't then
      That made you break° this enterprise to me?
      When you durst do it, then you were a man.
         I have given suck, and know
      How tender 'tis to love the babe that milks me:
      I would, while it was smiling in my face,
      Have plucked my nipple from his boneless gums,
      And dashed the brains out, had I so sworn as you
      Have done to this.

Macbeth.   If we should fail?

Lady M.   We fail?
      But° screw your courage to the sticking-place°,
      And we'll not fail. When Duncan is asleep

Break: broach. *But:* only. *Sticking-place:* the notch on a crossbow to keep the bowstring taut.

[Lady M.] His two chamberlains°
   Will I with wine and wassail° so convince°.
   What cannot you and I perform upon
   His spongy° officers, who shall bear the guilt
   Of our great quell°?

Macbeth.   Will it not be received,
   When we have marked with blood those sleepy two
   Of his own chamber, and used their very daggers,
   That they have done 't?

Lady M.   Who dares receive it other°,
   As we shall make our griefs and clamor roar
   Upon his death?

Macbeth.   I am settled, and bend up
   Each corporal agent to this terrible feat.
   Away, and mock the time° with fairest show:
   False face must hide what the false heart doth know.

They exit.

Chamberlains: personal attendants. *Wassail:* carousing. *Convince:* overpower.
Spongy: soaked with drink. *Quell:* murder. *Other:* otherwise. *Mock the time:*
deceive everyone.

Act II, Scene 1.
Inverness. Inner court of Macbeth's castle.

Enter Banquo and Fleance with a torch.

Banquo. How goes the night, boy?

Fleance. The moon is down; I have not heard the clock.

Banquo. And she goes down at twelve.

Fleance.   I take't, 'tis later, sir.

Banquo. Hold, take my sword. There's husbandry° in heaven.
　　Their candles are all out. Take thee that too.
　　A heavy summons° lies like lead upon me,
　　And yet I would not sleep.

Enter Macbeth and a servant with a torch.

Banquo. Give me my sword! Who's there?

Macbeth. A friend.

Banquo.   !!   All's well.
　　I dreamt last night of the three weird sisters:
　　To you they have showed some truth.
　　Yet, when we can entreat an hour to serve,
　　We would spend it in some words upon that business,
　　If you would grant the time.

Husbandry: frugality. *Summons:* call to sleep.

17

Macbeth.   I think not of them.

Banquo.   At your kind'st leisure.

Macbeth. Good repose the while!

Banquo. Thanks, sir. The like to you!

Exit Banquo and Fleance.

Macbeth. Go bid thy mistress, when my drink is ready,
    She strike upon the bell. Get thee to bed.

Exit servant.

Macbeth. Is this a dagger which I see before me,
    The handle toward my hand? Come, let me clutch thee.
    I have thee not, fatal vision, sensible°
    To feeling as to sight, or art thou but
    A dagger of the mind, a false creation,
    Proceeding from the heat-oppressèd brain?
    Thou marshal'st me the way that I was going;
    And such an instrument I was to use. *[A bell rings]*
    I go, and it is done: the bell invites me.
    Hear it not, Duncan, for it is a knell
    That summons thee to heaven, or to hell.

He exits.

Act II, Scene 2.
Same location.

Enter Lady Macbeth.

Sensible: perceptible.

Lady M. That which had made them drunk hath made me bold;
    Hark! Peace!
  It was the owl that shrieked, the fatal bellman°,
  Which gives the stern'st good-night. He is about it.
  The doors are open, and the surfeited grooms
  Do mock their charge with snores. I have drugged their
    possets°.

Macbeth. [Offstage]   Who's there? What, ho?

Lady M. Alack, I am afraid they have awaked
  And 'tis not done! I laid their daggers ready;
  He could not miss 'em. Had he not resembled
  My father as he slept, I had don't.

Enter Macbeth.

Lady M.   My husband!

Macbeth. I have done the deed. Didst thou not hear a noise?

Lady M. I heard the owl scream and the crickets cry.
  Did not you speak?

Macbeth.   When?

Lady M.   Now.

Macbeth.   As I descended?

Lady M. Ay.

Fatal bellman: town crier who would ring a bell at midnight outside the cell of prisoners condemned for execution in the morning. *Possets*: night cap of wine and hot milk.

Macbeth. Hark! Who lies in th' second chamber?

Lady M. Donalbain.

Macbeth.   This is a sorry° sight.

Lady M. A foolish thought, to say a sorry sight.

Macbeth. There's one did laugh in 's sleep, and one cried
    "Murder!"
    That they did wake each other. I stood and heard them.
    But they did say their prayers, and addressed them
    Again to sleep.

Lady M. There are two lodged together.

Macbeth. One cried "G-d bless us!" and "Amen" the other,
    As they had seen me with these hangman's° hands:
    List'ning their fear, I could not say "Amen,"
    When they did say "G-d bless us!"

Lady M. Consider it not so deeply.

Macbeth. But wherefore could not I pronounce "Amen?"
    I had most need of blessing, and "Amen" stuck in my throat.

Lady M. These deeds must not be thought
    After these ways; so, it will make us mad.

Macbeth. Methought I heard a voice cry "Sleep no more!
    Macbeth does murder sleep. Sleep no more!

Sorry: miserable. *Hangman's:* executioner's.

20

Macbeth. Glamis hath murdered sleep, and therefore Cawdor
    Shall sleep no more: Macbeth shall sleep no more."

Lady M. You do unbend° your noble strength, to think
    So brainsickly of things. Go get some water,
    And wash this filthy witness° from your hand.
    Why did you bring these daggers from the place?
    They must lie there: go carry them, and smear
    The sleepy grooms with blood.

Macbeth.   I'll go no more.
    I am afraid to think what I have done;
    Look on 't again I dare not.

Lady M.   Infirm of purpose!
    Give me the daggers. The sleeping and the dead
    Are but as pictures. If he do bleed,
    I'll gild° the faces of the grooms withal,
    For it must seem their guilt.

She exits and there is a knocking heard offstage.

Macbeth.   Whence is that knocking?
    How is't with me, when every noise appalls me?
    What hands are here? Ha! They pluck out mine eyes!
    Will all great Neptune's ocean wash this blood
    Clean from my hand? No: this my hand will rather
    The multitudinous seas incarnadine°,
    Making the green° one red.

Enter Lady Macbeth.

Unbend: relax. *Witness*: evidence. *Gild*: paint. *Incarnadine*: become blood red.
Green: ocean.

Lady M. My hands are of your color, but I shame
   To wear a heart so white. *[knock]* I hear a knocking.
   Retire we to our chamber.
   Be not lost so poorly° in your thoughts.

Macbeth. To know my deed, 'twere best not know myself.
   [knock] Wake Duncan with thy knocking! I would thou
   couldst!

They exit.

Act II, Scene 3.
Same location.

Enter the Porter. Knocking continues.

Porter. Here's a knocking indeed! If a man were porter of hell
   gate, he have old turning the key. *[knock]* Knock, knock,
   knock! Who's there, in th' name of Beelzebub? Here's a
   farmer, that hanged himself on the expectation of plenty.
   [knock] Knock, knock, knock! Never at quiet! What are
   you? *[knock]* Anon, anon! *[Opens an entrance just off
   stage.]* I pray you, remember the porter.

Enter Macduff and Lennox.

Macduff. Was it so late, friend, ere you went to bed,
   That you do lie so late?

Porter. Faith, sir, we were carousing till the second cock°: and
   drink, sir, is a great provoker of three things.

Poorly: weakly.   *Second cock:* 3:00 a.m.

Macduff. What three things does drink especially provoke?

Porter. Marry, sir, nose-painting, sleep, and urine. Sir, it
   provokes and unprovokes; it provokes the desire, but it takes
   away the performance: makes him stand to and not stand to;
   in conclusion, equivocates him in a sleep, and giving him the
   lie, leaves him.

Macduff. I believe drink gave thee the lie° last night.

Porter. That it did, sir.

Macduff. Is thy master stirring?

Enter Macbeth.

Macduff. Our knocking has awaked him. Here he comes.

Lennox. Good morrow, noble sir.

Macbeth.   Good morrow, both.

Macduff. Is the King stirring, worthy Thane?

Macbeth.   Not yet.

Macduff. He did command me to call timely° on him:
   I have almost slipped° the hour.

Macbeth.   I'll bring you to him.

Lie: a pun on making him a liar and lying him out flat.   *Timely*: early.   *Slipped*: let
slip.

Macduff. I'll make so bold to call, for 'tis my limited service°.

Exit Macduff.

Lennox. Goes the King hence today?

Macbeth.   He does: he did appoint so.

Lennox. The night has been unruly. Where we lay,
　　Our chimneys were blown down, and, as they say,
　　Lamentings heard in th' air, strange screams of death,
　　And prophesying with accents terrible
　　Of dire combustion° and confused events
　　New hatched to th' woeful time.

Macbeth.   'Twas a rough night.

Lennox. My young remembrance cannot parallel a fellow to it.

Enter Macduff.

Macduff. Most sacrilegious murder hath broke ope
　　The Lord's annointed temple, and stole thence
　　The life o' th' building.

Macbeth.   What is 't you say? The life?

Lennox. Mean you his Majesty?

Macduff. Approach the chamber, and destroy your sight;
　　See, and the speak yourselves. Awake, awake!

Service: duty.   *Combustion:* tumult.

Exit Macbeth and Lennox.

Macduff. Ring the alarum bell. Murder and Treason!
  Banquo and Donalbain! Malcolm! Awake!
  Shake off this downy sleep, death's counterfeit°,
  And look on death itself! Up, up, and see
  The great doom's image! Ring the bell! *[Bell rings]*

Lady Macbeth enters.

Lady M. What's the business,
  That such a hideous trumpet calls to parley
  The sleepers of the house? Speak, speak!

Macduff.   O gentle lady,
  'Tis not for you to hear what I can speak:
  The repetition°, in a woman's ear,
  Would murder as it fell.

Enter Banquo.

  O Banquo, Banquo! Our royal master's murdered.

Lady M.   Woe, alas!
  What, in our house?

Banquo.   Too cruel anywhere.
  Dear Duff, I prithee, contradict thyself,
  And say it is not so.

Enter Macbeth, Lennox, and Ross.

Counterfeit: imitation.   *Repetition*: report.

25

Macbeth. Had I but died an hour before this chance,
   I had lived a blessèd time.

Enter Malcolm and Donalbain.

Donalbain. What is amiss?

Macbeth.   You are, and do not know 't.
   The spring, the head, the fountain of your blood
   Is stopped; the very source of it is stopped.

Macduff. Your royal father's murdered.

Malcolm.   O, by whom?

Lennox. Those of his chamber, as it seemed, had done 't:
   Their hands and faces were all badged° with blood;
   So were their daggers, which unwiped we found
   Upon their pillows.

Macbeth. O, yet I do not repent me of my fury,
   That I did kill them.

Macduff.   Wherefore did you so?

Macbeth. Who can be wise, amazed°, temp'rate and furious
   in a moment? No man. Here lay Duncan
   His silver skin laced with his golden blood, there the
      murders,
   Steeped in the color of their trade, their daggers
   Unmannerly breeched with gore. Who could refrain?
   That had a heart to love?

Badged: smeared.   *Amazed*: bewildered.

26

Lady M.   Help me hence, ho!

Macduff. Look to the lady.

Malcolm.[Aside to Donalbain] What should be spoken here,
    Where our fate, hid in an auger-hole°
    May rush, and seize us? Let's away:
    Our tears are not yet brewed.

Malcolm. [Aside to Donalbain] Nor our strong sorrow
    Upon the foot of motion°.

Banquo.   Look to the lady.

Lady Macbeth is carried out.

Banquo. And when we have our naked frailties hid°,
    That suffer in exposure, let us meet
    And question° this most bloody piece of work,
    To know it further. Fears and scruples° shake us.
    In the great hand of G-d I stand, and thence
    Against the undivulged pretense° I fight
    Of treasonous malice.

Macduff.   And so do I.

All.   So all.

Macbeth. Let's briefly put on manly readiness,
    And meet in th' hall together.

Auger-hole: unsuspected place. *Upon...motion: i.e.* we haven't the time for tears or
expressing our sorrow in action. *Naked frailties hid:* poor bodies clothed. *Question:*
discuss. *Scruples:* suspicions. *Pretense:* purpose.

All. Well contented.

Exit all but Malcolm and Donalbain.

Malcolm. What will you do? Let's not consort with them.
   To show an unfelt sorrow is an office°
   Which the false man does easy. I'll to England.

Donalbain. To Ireland, I: our separated fortune
   Shall keep us both the safer. Where we are
   There's daggers in men's smiles; the near in blood,
   The near bloody.

Malcolm.   This murderous shaft that's shot
   Hath not yet lighted, and our safest way
   Is to avoid the aim. Therefore to horse;
   And let us not be dainty of° leave-taking,
   But shift away. There's warrant° in that theft
   Which steals itself° when there's no mercy left.

They exit.

Act II, Scene 4.
Inverness. Outside Macbeth's castle.

Enter Ross and Macduff.

Ross. How goes the world, sir, now?

Macduff. Malcolm and Donalbain, the king's two sons,
   Are stol'n away and fled, which puts upon them
   Suspicion of the deed.

Office: action. *Dainty of*: fussy about. *Warrant*: reason. *Steals itself*: leaves
shrewdly.

Ross.   Then 'tis most like
  The sovereignty will fall upon Macbeth.

Macduff. He is already named°, and gone to Scone
  To be invested°.

Ross.   Where is Duncan's body?

Macduff. Carried to Colmekill.

Ross.   Will you come to Scone?

Macduff. No cousin, I'll to Fife.

Ross.   Well, I will thither.

Macduff. Well, may you see things well done there. Adieu,
  Lest our old robes sit easier than our new!

Ross. Farewell.

They exit.

Named: elected.   *Invested*: instated as king.

Act III, Scene 1.
Forres. The palace.

Enter Banquo.

Banquo. Thou hast it now: King, Cawdor, Glamis, all,
  As the weird women promised, and I fear
  Thou play'st most foully for 't. But hush, no more!

*Sennet ° sounded. Enter Macbeth as King, Lady Macbeth,
Lennox, Ross, Lords, and Attendants.*

Macbeth. Here's our chief guest.
  Tonight we hold a solemn° supper, sir,
  And I'll request your presense.

Banquo.   Let your Highness
  Command upon me, to the which my duties
  Are with a most indissoluble tie for ever knit.

Macbeth.   Fail not our feast.

Banquo. My lord, I will not.

Macbeth. We hear our bloody cousins are bestowed°
  In England and in Ireland, not confessing
  Their cruel parricide, filling their hearers
  With strange invention°. But of that tomorrow,
  When withal we shall have cause of state
  Craving us jointly°. Hie you to horse. Adieu,
  Till you return at night. Goes Fleance with you?

Sennet: trumpet call. *Solemn*: ceremonious. *Bestowed*: taking refuge. *Invention*:
lies. *Cause...jointly:* official business requiring our attention.

Banquo. Ay, my lord: our time does call upon 's.

Macbeth. I wish your horses swift and sure of foot,
   And so I do commend you to their backs.
   Farewell. *[Exit Banquo]*
   Let every man be master of his time
   Till seven at night. To make society
   The sweeter welcome, we will keep ourself
   Till supper-time alone. While° then, G-d be with you!

Exit all but Macbeth and an attendant.

   Sirrah°, a word with you: attend° those men our pleasure?

Attendant. They are, my lord, without° the palace gate.

Macbeth. Bring them before us. *[Attendant exits]*
   Our fears in Banquo stick deep,
   And in his royalty of nature° reigns that
   Which would° be feared. He chid the sisters,
   When first they put the name of king upon me,
   And bade them speak to him; then profetlike
   They hailed him father to a line of kings.
   For Banquo's issue have I filed° my mind;
   For them the gracious Duncan have I murdered;
   To make them kings? The seeds of Banquo kings?
   Rather than so, come, fate, into the list°,
   And champion me to th' utterance°! Who's there?

Enter Two Murderers.

While: until. *Sirrah:* common address to inferiors. *Attend:* await. *Without:* outside.
Royalty of nature: natural ability to lead. *Would:* should. *Filed:* defiled. *List:* arena.
Champion me to th' utterance: give me a valiant opponent to the end.

[Macbeth.] Was it not yesterday we spoke together?

First Murderer. It was, so please your Highness.

Macbeth.   Well then, now
   Have you considered of my speeches? Know
   That it was he in the times past, which held you
   so under fortune°, which you thought had been
   Our innocent self. Well, thus did Banquo!

Second Murderer. Ay, my liege.

Macbeth.   Do you find
   Your patience so predominant in your nature,
   That you can let this go? Are you so gospeled°,
   To pray for this good man and for his issue,
   Whose heavy hand hath bowed you to the grave
   and beggared yours for ever?

First Murderer.   We are men, my liege.

Macbeth. Ay, in the catalogue ye go° for men;
   Now if you have a station in the file,
   Not in th' worst rank of manhood, say 't,
   And I will put that business in your bosoms
   Whose execution takes your enemy off,
   Grapples you to the heart and love of us,
   Who wear our health but sickly in his life°,
   Which in his death were perfect.

Held you...fortune: kept you from good fortune.   *Gospeled:* made weak by religion.
Go: pass.   *In his life*: while he lives.

Second Murderer.   I am one, my liege,
   Whom the vile blows and buffets of the world
   Hath so incensed that I am reckless what
   I do to spite the world.

First Murderer.   And I another
   So weary with disasters, tugged with fortune,
   That I would set° my life on any chance,
   To mend it or be rid on 't.

Macbeth. Both of you know Banquo was your enemy.

Both Murderers.   True, my lord.

Macbeth. So is he mine: and though I could
   With barefaced power sweep him from my sight
                       Yet I must not,
   For certain friends are both his and mine.
   I too your assistance do make love,
   Masking the business to the common eye.

Second Murderer. We shall, my lord, perform what you
   command us.

First Murderer. Though our lives—

Macbeth.   Your spirits shine through you.
   Within this hour at most
   I will advise you where to plant yourselves.
   Fleance his son, that keeps him company,

Set: risk.

[Macbeth.] Must embrace the fate of that dark hour.
    Resolve yourselves apart°:
    I'll come to you anon.

Second Murderer.   We are resolved, my lord.

Macbeth. I'll call upon you straight°. Abide within. *[They exit]*
    It is concluded: Banquo, thy soul's flight,
    If it find heaven, must find it out tonight.

Macbeth exits.

Act III, Scene 2.
Same location.

Enter Lady Macbeth and a Servant.

Lady M. Is Banquo gone from court?

Servant. Ay, madam, but returns again tonight.

Lady M. Say to the King, I would attend his leisure
    For a few words.

Servant.   Madam, I will.

Exit Servant.

Resolve yourselves apart: decide on your own.   *Straight:* immediately.

Lady M.   Nought's had, all's spent,
    Where our desire is got without content:
    'Tis safer to be that which we destroy
    Than by destruction dwell in doubtful joy.

Enter Macbeth.

Lady M. How now, my lord? What's done is done.

Macbeth. Duncan is in his grave.
    After life's fitful fever he sleeps well.

Lady M.   Come on.
    Gentle my lord, sleek° o'er your rugged° looks;
    Be bright and jovial among our guests tonight.

Macbeth. So shall I, love; and so, I pray, be you.
    We must make our faces vizards° to our hearts,
    Disguising what they are.

Lady M.   You must leave this.

Macbeth. O, full of scorpions is my mind, dear wife!
    Thou know'st that Banquo, and his Fleance, lives.

Lady M. What's to be done?

Macbeth. Be innocent of the knowledge, dearest chuck°,
    Till thou applaud the deed.
    Things had begun make strong themselves by ill:
    So prithee, go with me. *[They exit.]*

Sleek: smooth.   *Rugged:* rough.   *Vizards:* masks.   *Chuck:* chick (term of endearment)

Act III, Scene 3.
Forres. A park near the palace.

Enter Three Murderers.

First Murderer. But who did bid thee join with us?

Third Murder.   Macbeth.

Second Murderer. He needs not our mistrust; since he delivers
    Our offices and what we have to do
    To the direction just°.

First Murderer.   Then stand with us.

Third Murderer. Hark! I hear the horses.

Banquo. [Offstage] Give us a light there, ho!

Second Murderer.   Then 'tis he. The rest
    That are within the note of expectation°
    Already are in th' court.

First Murderer.   His horses go about.

Third Murder. But he goes usually from hence to the palace
    gate.

Enter Banquo and Fleance with a torch.

To the direction just: according to Macbeth's directions.   *Note of expectation*: list of
expected guests.

Second Murderer. A light, a light!

First Murderer.   Stand to 't.

Banquo. It will be rain tonight.

First Murderer.   Let it come down!

They attack Banquo.

Banquo. O, treachery! Fly, good Fleance, fly, fly, fly!

Exit Fleance.

    Thou mayst revenge. O slave! *[Dies]*

Third Murder. Who did strike out the light?

First Murderer.   Was 't not the way°?

Third Murderer. There's but one down. The son is fled.

Second Murderer. We have lost best half of our affair.

First Murderer. Well, let's away and say how much is done.

They exit

Way: appropriate thing to do.

Act III, Scene 4.
Forres. The palace.

Banquet is prepared. Enter Macbeth, Lady Macbeth, Ross, Lennox, Lords, and Attendants.

Macbeth. You know your own degrees°; sit down:
    At first and last, the hearty welcome.

Lords. Thanks to your Majesty.

Macbeth. Ourself will mingle with society°
    And play the humble host.

Lady M. Pronounce it for me, sir, to all our friends,
    For my heart speaks they are welcome.

Enter First Murderer.

Macbeth. [Goes to the Murderer] There's blood upon thy face.

Murderer. 'Tis Banquo's then.

Macbeth. Is he dispatched?

Murderer. My lord, his throat is cut; that I did for him.

Macbeth. Thou art the best o' th' cutthroats.

Murderer. Most royal sir, Fleance is 'scaped.

Degrees: rank. *Society:* our company.

Macbeth. [Aside] Then comes my fit again:
  I had else been perfect! Get thee gone.
  Tomorrow we'll hear ourselves° again.

Exit Murderer.

Lady M. My royal lord,
  You do not give the cheer°.

Enter Ghost of Banquo and sits in Macbeth's place.

Macbeth.   Sweet remembrancer°!
  Now good digestion wait on appetite,
  And health on both!

Lennox.   May it please your Highness sit...

Ross. Please 't our Highness to grace us with your royal
  company?

Macbeth. The table's full.

Lennox.   Here is a place reserved, sir.

Macbeth. Where?

Lennox. Here, my good lord. What is 't that moves your
  highness?

Macbeth. Which of you have done this?

Lords.   What, my good lord?

Hear ourselves: talk this over.   *Cheer:* feeling of welcome.   *Remembrancer:* reminder.

Macbeth. Thou canst not say I did it. Never shake thy
    Gory locks at me.

Ross. Gentlemen, rise, his Highness is not well.

Lady M. Sit, worthy friends. My lord is often thus,
    And hath been from his youth. Pray you, keep seat.
    The fit is momentary. If much you note him,
    You shall offend° him and extend his passion°
    Feed, and regard him not.
    [Softly, to Macbeth] Are you a man?

Macbeth. Ay, and a bold one, that dare look on that
    Which might appall the devil.

Lady M.   O proper stuff!
    This is the very painting of your fear.

Macbeth.   Prithee, see there!
    Behold! Look! Lo! How say you?
    Why, what care I? If thou canst nod, speak too.

Exit Ghost.

Lady M. What, quite unmanned in folly?

Macbeth. If I stand here, I saw him.

Lady M.   Fie, for shame!
    My worthy lord, your noble friends do lack you.

Offend him: upset.   *Extend his passion:* prolong his fit.

Macbeth.   I do forget.
   Do not muse at me, my most worthy friends;
   I have a strange infirmity, which is nothing
   To those that know me. Come, love and health to all!
   Then I'll sit down. Give me some wine, fill full.

Enter Ghost.

Macbeth. I drink to th' general joy o' th' whole table,
   And to our dear friend, Banquo, whom we miss;
   Would he were here! To all and him we thirst°,
   And all to all°.

Lords.   Our duties, and the pledge.

Macbeth. Avaunt! And quit my sight! Let the earth hide thee!
   Thy bones are marrowless, thy blood is cold.
   Hence, horrible shadow! Unreal mock'ry, hence!

Ghost exits.

Macbeth. Why, so: being gone, I am a man again.
   Pray you, sit still.

Lady M. [Softly to Macbeth] You have displaced the mirth,
   Broke the good meeting with most admired° disorder.

Macbeth. Can such things be? How can you behold such sights
   And keep the natural ruby of your cheeks,
   When mine is blanched with fear?

Ross.   What sights, my lord?

Thirst: eagerly drink. *All to all*: only good should come to all. *Admired:* amazing.

Lady M. I pray you, speak not: he grows worse and worse;
    Question enrages him: at once, good night. Go at once.

Lennox.   Good night; and better health attend his Majesty!

Lady M. A kind good night to all!

Lords exit.

Macbeth. It will have blood, they say: blood will have blood.
    Stones have been known to move and trees to speak.

Macbeth. How say'st thou, that Macduff denies his person
    At our great bidding? I will, to the weird sisters:
    More shall they speak, for now I am bent° to know
    By the worst means the worst. For mine own good
    All causes° shall give way. I am in blood
    Stepped in so far that, should I wade no more,
    Returning were as tedious as go o'er.
    Strange things have I in head that will to hand,
    Which must be acted ere they may be scanned°.

Lady M. You lack the sense of all natures°, sleep.

Macbeth. Come, we'll to sleep. We are yet but young in deed°.

They exit.

Bent: determined.   *Causes*: considerations.   *Scanned*: studied.   *You lack...natures*:
you lack the desire of self-preservation as seen in all living creatures.   Young in
deed: new at crime.

42

Act III, Scene 5 is cut.

Act III, Scene 6.
Somewhere in Scotland.

Enter Lennox and a Lord.

Lennox. Macduff lives in disgrace. Sir, can you tell
   Where he bestows himself?

Lord.   The son of Duncan,
   From whom this tyrant holds the due of birth°,
   Lives in the English court, and is received
   Of the most pious Edward° with such grace
   That the malevolence of fortune nothing
   Takes from his high respect. Thither Macduff
   Is gone to pray the holy King, upon his aid°
   To wake° Northumberland and warlike Siward.
   And this report hath so exasperate the King that he
   Prepares for some attempt of war.

Lennox.   Sent he to Macduff?

Lord. He did: and with an absolute "Sir, not I,"
   The cloudy° messenger turns me his back,
   And hums, as who should say, "You'll rue the time
   That clogs° me with this answer."

Holds the...birth: withholds his birthright (the crown). *Edward:* Edward the Confessor
(reigned 1042-1066). *Upon his aid:* on Malcolm's behalf. *Awake:* arouse to arms.
Cloudy: scowling. *Clog:* burdens.

Lennox. Some holy angel
　　Fly to the court of England and unfold
　　His message ere he come, that a swift blessing
　　may soon return to this our suffering country
　　Under a hand accursed!

Lord. I'll send my prayers with him.

They exit.

Act IV, Scene 1.
A cave with a boiling cauldron.

Thunder. Enter the Three Witches.

First Witch. Thrice and brinded° cat hath mewed.

Second Witch. Thrice and once the hedge-pig° whined.

Third Witch. Harpier° cries. 'Tis time, 'tis time.

All. Double, double, toil and trouble;
　　Fire burn and cauldron bubble.

Second Witch. Fillet° of a fenny° snake;
　　In the cauldron boil and bake.

All. Double, double, toil and trouble;
　　Fire burn and cauldron bubble.

Brinded: streaked. *Hedge-pig*: hedgehog. *Harpier*: a helpful spirit. *Fillet:* slice.
Fenny: swamp.

First Witch. Cool it with a baboon's blood,
    Then the charm is fire and good.

Third Witch. By the pricking of my thumbs,
    Something wicked this way comes:

First Witch. Open, locks—

Third Witch. Whoever knocks!

Enter Macbeth.

Macbeth. How now, you secret, black, and midnight hags!
    What is 't you do?

All. A deed without a name.

Macbeth. I conjure you, by that which you profess,
    Howe'er you come to know it, answer me:
    Answer me to what I ask you.

First Witch.   Speak.

Second Witch.   Demand.

Third Witch. We'll answer.

All.   Come, high or low,
    Thyself and office deftly show!

Thunder. Enter First Apparition: an Armed Head.

Macbeth. Tell me, thou knowest power—

First Apparition. Macbeth! Macbeth! Macbeth! Beware
        Macduff!
    Beware the Thane of Fife. Dismiss me: enough.

Apparition descends.

Macbeth. Whate'er thou art, for thy good caution thanks.
    Thou hast harped° my fear aright. But one word more—

First Witch. He will not be commanded. Here's another,
    More potent than the first.

Thunder. Second Apparition: a Bloody Child.

Second Apparition. Macbeth! Macbeth! Macbeth!

Macbeth. Had I three ears, I'd hear thee.

Second Apparition. Be bloody, bold and resolute!
        Laugh to scorn
    The pow'r of man, for none of woman born
    Shall harm Macbeth.

Apparition descends.

Macbeth. Then live, Macduff: what need I fear of thee?
    But yet I'll make assurance double sure,
    And take a bond of fate°. Thou shalt not live!

*Thunder. Third Apparition: a Child Crowned °,
with a tree in his hand.*

Harped: hit upon.   *Take a bond of fate*: make the prophesy come true.   *Child Crowned*: signifying Malcolm.

Macbeth. What is this, that rises like the issue of a king?

All. Listen, but speak not to 't.

Third Apparition. Macbeth shall never vanquished be until
   Great Birnam Wood to high Dunsinane Hill
   Shall come against him.

Apparition descends.

Macbeth.   That will never be.
   Who can impress° the forest, bid the tree
   Unfix his earth-bound root? Sweet bodements°, good!
   Yet my heart throbs to know one thing. Tell me, if your art
   Can tell so much: shall Banquo's issue° ever
   Reign in this kingdom?

All.   Seek to know no more.

Macbeth. I will be satisfied. Deny me this,
   And an eternal curse fall on you! Let me know.
   Why sinks that cauldron. *[Noise]* And what noise° is this?

The Witches dance and vanish.

Macbeth. Where are they? Gone? Let this pernicious hour
   Stand aye accursèd in the calendar!

Enter Lennox.

Lennox. Macduff is fled to England.

Impress: control. *Bodements*: prophecies. *Issue*: children. *Noise*: music.

Macbeth.   Fled to England?

Lennox. Ay, my good lord.

Macbeth indicates Lennox is to leave. Lennox does so.

Macbeth. The castle of Macduff I will surprise°;
    Seize upon Fife; give to th' edge of th' sword
    His wife, his babes, and all unfortunate souls
    That trace him in his line°. No boasting like a fool;
    This deed I'll do before this purpose cool.

He exits.

Act IV, Scene 2.
Macduff's Castle.

Enter Lady Macduff, her son, and Ross.

Lady Macduff. What had he done, to make Macduff fly to
    England?

Ross. You must have patience, madam.

Lady Macduff.   He had none:
    His flight was madness. When our actions do not,
    Our fears do make us traitors.

Ross. You know not whether it was his wisdom or his fear.

Surprise: attack without warning. *Line:* lineage.

Lady Macduff. Wisdom! To leave his wife, to leave his babes,
   His mansion and his titles°, in a place
   From whence himself does fly? He loves us not.
   All is the fear and nothing is the love.

Ross.   My dearest coz°,
   I pray you, school° yourself. But, for your husband,
   He is noble, wise, judicious, and best knows
   The fits o' th' season°. I dare not speak much further:

Lady Macbeth. Fathered he is, yet he's fatherless.

Ross. I am so much a fool, should I stay longer,
   It would be my disgrace and your discomfort°.
   I'll take my leave at once. *[Ross exits]*

Lady Macduff.   Sirrah°, your father's dead:
   And what will you do now? How will you live?

Son. Was my father a traitor, mother?

Lady Macduff. Ay, that he was.

Son. What is a traitor?

Lady Macduff. Why, one that swears and lies°.

Son. And be all traitors that do so?

Lady Macduff. Every one that does so is a traitor, and must be
   hanged.

Titles: possessions. *Coz*: cousin. *School*: control. *Season*: disturbances of the time.
It would...discomfort: *i.e.* I should weep. *Sirrah*: in this instance used as an
affectionate address. *Lies*: breaks a vow.

Son. Who must hang them?

Lady Macduff. Why, the honest men.

Son. Then the liars and swearers are fools; for there are liars
and swearers enow° to beat the honest men and hang up
them.

Enter a Messenger.

Messenger. Bless you, fair dame! I am not to you known,
Though in your state of honor, I am perfect°.
I doubt° some danger does approach you nearby:
If you will take a homely° man's advice,
Be not found here; hence, with your little ones.
Heaven preserve you! I dare abide no longer. *[He exits]*

Lady Macduff.   Whither should I fly?
I have done no harm. But I remember now
I am in this earthly world, where to do harm
Is often laudable, to do good sometime
Accounted dangerous folly.

Enter Murderers.

First Murderer. Where is your husband?

Lady Macduff. I hope, in no place so unsanctified
Where such as thou mayst find him.

Second Murderer.   He's a traitor!

Enow: enough. *In...perfect*: I am aware of your distinguished position. *Doubt*: fear.
Homely: plain.

Son. Thou liest, thou shag-eared° villain!

Second Murderer. What, you egg. Young fry° of treachery!
[Stabs the son]

Son. He has killed me, mother. Run away, I pray you! *[He dies]*

*Exit Lady Macduff crying "Murder!"—followed by
Murderers.*

Act IV, Scene 3.
England. Before King Edward's palace.

Enter Malcolm and Macduff.

Malcolm. Let us seek out some desolate shade, and there
    Weep our sad bosoms empty.

Macduff.   Let us rather
    Hold fast the mortal° sword, and like good men
    Bestride our down-fall'n birthdom°.

Malcolm. You may deserve of him through me°; and wisdom°
    To offer up a weak, poor, innocent lamb
    T' appease an angry god.

Macduff.   I am not treacherous.

Shag-eared: shaggy hair hanging over the ears. *Fry:* spawn. *Mortal:* deadly.
Bestride...birthdom: stand over our native land. *You may deserve... me:* you may find
favor with Macbeth by betraying me. *Wisdom:* it may be smart.

Malcolm. But Macbeth is. Why in that rawness° left you wife
    and child,
    You may be rightly just, whatever I shall think.

Macduff. For the whole space that's in the tyrant's grasp
    And the rich East to boot.

Malcolm. Be not offended:
    I speak not as in absolute fear of you.
    I think our country sinks beneath the yoke;
    It weeps, it bleeds, and each new day a gash
    Is added to her wounds.

Macduff.   Not in the legions
    Of horrid hell can come a devil more damned
    In evils to top Macbeth. O Scotland, Scotland!

Malcolm. If such a one be fit to govern, speak:
    I am as I have spoken.

Macduff.   Fit to govern!
    No, not to live. O nation miserable!
    With an untitled tyrant bloody-sceptered,
    When shalt thou see thy wholesome days again,
    Since that the truest issue of thy throne
    By his own interdiction° stands accursed,
    And does blaspheme his breed?° Thy royal father
    Was a most sainted king: the queen that bore thee,
    Oft'ner upon her knees than on her feet,
    Died° every day she lived. Fare thee well!

Rawness: vulnerable position. *Interdiction:* curse. *Breed:* ancestry. *Died: i.e.*
prepared for heaven.

Macduff. These evils thou repeat'st upon thyself
 Hath banished me from Scotland. O my breast,
 Thy hope ends here.

Malcolm.   Macduff, this noble passion,
 Child of integrity, hath from my soul
 Wiped the black scruples°, reconciled my thoughts
 To thy good truth and honor. Devilish Macbeth
 By many of these trains° hath sought to win me
 Into his power; and modest wisdom° plucks me
 From over-credulous haste: but G-d above
 Deal between thee and me!

Enter Ross.

Ross. Sir!

Macduff. Stands Scotland where it did?

Ross.   Alas, poor country!
 Almost afraid to know itself! It cannot
 Be called our mother but our grave;
 Where sighs and groans, and shrieks that rent the air,
 Are made, not marked°; where violent sorrow seems
 A modern ecstasy°.

Macduff.   O, relation
 Too nice°, and yet too true!

Malcolm.   What's the newest grief?

Scruples: fears. *Trains:* plots. *Wisdom:* prudence. *Marked:* noticed. *Modern ecstasy:* every day emotions. *Nice:* precise.

53

Macduff. How does my wife?

Ross. Why, well.

Macduff.　　　　And all my children?

Ross.　　　　　　　　Well too.

Macduff. The tyrant has not battered at their peace?

Ross. No; they were well at peace when I did leave 'em.

Macduff. Be not a niggard of your speech°: how goes 't?

Ross. Let not your ears despise my tongue for ever,
　　Which shall possess them with the heaviest sound
　　That ever yet they heard.

Macduff.　　　　　　Humh! I guess at it.

Ross. Your castle is surprised; your wife and babes
　　Savagely slaughtered. To relate the manner
　　Were, on the quarry° of these murdered deer,
　　To add the death of you.

Malcolm.　　　　　Merciful heaven! What, man!

Macduff. My children too?

Ross. Wife, children, servants, all that could be found.

Be not...speech: *i.e.* don't try to put me off.　*Quarry*: heap of slaughtered bodies.

Macduff. And I must be from thence!

Malcolm.   Be comforted.
    Let's make us med'cines of our great revenge,
    To cure this deadly grief. Dispute it° like a man.

Macduff.   I shall do so;
    But I must also feel it as a man. Sinful Macduff,
    They were all struck for thee! Heaven rest them now!

Malcolm. Be this the whetstone of your sword. Let grief
    Convert to anger; blunt not the heart, enrage it.

Macduff. O, I could play the woman with mine eyes,
    And braggart with my tongue!
    Bring thou this fiend of Scotland and myself;
    Within my sword's length set him. If he 'scape,
    Heaven forgive him too!

Malcolm.   This time goes manly.
    Come, go we to the King. Macbeth
    Is ripe for shaking, and the pow'rs above
    Put on their instruments°.
    The night is long that never finds the day.

They exit.

Dispute it: fight against it. *Instruments*: armaments.

Act V, Scene 1.
Dunsinane. Macbeth's castle.

Enter a Doctor of Physic and a Waiting-Gentlewoman.

Gentlewoman. Since his majesty went into the field, I have seen her rise from her bed, throw her nightgown upon her, unlock her closet°, take forth paper, fold it, write upon 't, read it, afterwards seal it, and again return to bed; yet all this while in a most fast sleep.

Doctor. A great perturbation in nature, to receive at once the benefit of sleep and do the effects of watching°! In this slumb'ry agitation, besides her walking and other actual performances°, what, at any time, have you heard her say?

Gentlewoman. That, sir, which I will not report after her.

Doctor. You may to me, and 'tis most meet° you should.

Gentlewoman. Neither to you or anyone, having no witness to confirm my speech.

Enter Lady Macbeth with a taper.

Gentlewoman. Lo you, here she comes! This is her very guise°, and, upon my life, fast asleep! She has light by her continually. 'Tis her command.

Doctor. You see, her eyes are open...Look how she rubs her hands.

Closet: cabinet or chest.   *Do...of watching*: perform acts normally done while awake.
Performances: actions.   *Meet*: appropriate.   *Guise*: routine.

Gentlewoman. It is an accustomed action with her, to seem thus washing her hands: I have known her continue in his a quarter of an hour.

Lady M. Out, damned spot! Out, I say! One: two: why, then 'til time to do 't. Hell is murky. Fie, my lord, fie! A soldier, and afeard? What need we fear who knows it, when none can call our pow'r to accompt°? Yet who would have thought the old man to have had so much blood in him?

Doctor. Do you mark that?

Lady M. The Thane of Fife had a wife. Where is she now? What, will these hands ne'er be cleaned?

Doctor. Go to, go to! You have known what you should not.

Gentlewoman. She hath spoke what she should not, I am sure of that. Heaven knows what she has known.

Lady M. Here's the smell of the blood still. All the perfumes of Arabia will not sweeten this little hand. Oh, oh, oh!

Doctor. This disease is beyond my practice°.

Lady M. I tell you yet again, Banquo's buried. He cannot come out on 's° grave.

Doctor. Even so?

Accompt: accountability. *Practice:* professional ability. *On 's:* of his.

Lady M. To bed, to bed! There's knocking at the gate. Come,
   come, come, come, give me your hand! What's done cannot
   be undone. To bed, to bed, to bed!

Lady Macbeth exits.

Doctor. Will she go now to bed?

Gentlewoman. Directly.

Doctor. Foul whisp'rings are abroad. Unnatural deeds
   Do breed unnatural troubles. Look after her;
   Remove from her the means of all annoyance°,
   And still° keep eyes upon her. So good night.
   My mind she has mated° and amazed my sight:
   I think, but dare not speak.

Gentlewoman.   Good night, good doctor.

They exit.

Act V, Scene 2.

The country near Dunsinane.

*Drums and colors. Enter Menteth, Cathness, Angus, Lennox, and
Soldiers.*

Menteth. The English pow'r is near, led on by Malcolm,
   His uncle Siward and the good Macduff.
   Revenges burn in them; for their dear° causes
   Would to the bleeding and the grim alarm
   Excite the mortified man°.

Annoyance: (self) injury. *Still:* continuously. *Mated:* stupefied. *Dear:* heartfelt.
The mortified man: a dead man to join the battle.

Angus.   Near Birnam Wood
   Shall we well meet them; that way are they coming.

Cathness. Who knows if Donalbain be with his brother?

Lennox. For certain, sir, he is not.

Angus.   Now does he feel
   His secret murders sticking on his hands;
         Now does he feel his title
   Hang loose upon him, like a giant's robe
   Upon a dwarfish thief.

Cathness.   Well, march we on,
   To give obedience where 'tis truly owed.

Lennox. Make we our march towards Birnam.

They exit, marching.

                    Act V, Scene 3.
             Dunsinane. Macbeth's castle.

Enter Macbeth, Doctor, and Attendants.

Macbeth. Bring me no more reports: let them fly all!
   Till Birnam Wood remove to Dunsinane
   I cannot taint° with fear. What's the boy Malcolm?
   Was he not born of woman? The spirits have pronounced:
   "Fear not, Macbeth; no man that's born of woman
   Shall e'er have power upon thee." Then fly false thanes.

Taint: overcome.

59

Enter Servant.

Servant. There is ten thousand soldiers, sir.

Macbeth. What soldiers, patch°?

Servant. The English force, so please you.

Macbeth. Take thy face hence. *[Servant exits]*
        Seyton!—This push°
  Will cheer me ever, or disseat° me now.

Enter Seyton.

Seyton. What's your gracious pleasure?

Macbeth.   What news more?

Seyton. All is confirmed, my lord, which was reported.

Macbeth. I'll fight, till from my bones my flesh be hacked.
  Give me my armor. Send out more horses,
  Skirr° the country round.
  Hang those that talk of fear. Give me mine armor.
  How does your patient, doctor?

Doctor.   Not so sick, my lord,
  As she is troubled with thick-coming fancies
  That keep her from her rest.

Macbeth.   Cure her of that.
  Canst thou not minister to a mind diseased?

Patch: fool. *Push:* effort. *Disseat:* dethrone. *Skirr:* scour.

Doctor. The patient must minister to himself.

Macbeth. Throw physic° to the dogs, I'll none of it.
 Doctor, cast the water° of my land, find her disease.
 What rhubard, cyme, or what purgative drug,
 Would scour these English hence? Hear'st thou of them?

Doctor. Ay, my good lord; your royal preparation
 Makes us hear something.

Macbeth. Bring it after me.
 I will not be afraid of death and bane,
 Till Birnam forest come to Dunsinane.

Exit all but Doctor.

Doctor. Were I from Dunsinane away and clear,
 Profit again should hardly draw me here°.

Act V, Scene 4.
The Country near Birnam Wood.

*Drums and colors. Enter Malcolm, Siward, Macduff, Siward's
Son, Menteth, Caithness, Angus, Lennox, Ross, and Soldiers.*

Malcolm. Cousins, I hope the days are near at hand
 That chambers will be safe°.

Menteth.   We doubt in nothing°.

Physic: medical science. *Cast the water*: analyze the urine. *Profit...here*: no fee is
great enough to bring me back. *That chambers....safe*: all will be safe in their
bedrooms. *Nothing*: not at all.

Siward. What wood is this before us?

Menteth.   The Wood of Birnam.

Malcolm. Let every soldier hew him down a bough
    And bear 't before him. Thereby shall we shadow
    The numbers of our host, and make discovery°
    Err in report of us.

Soldiers.   It shall be done.

They exit, marching.

                        Act V, Scene 5.
                 Dunsinane. Macbeth's castle.

Drum and colors. Enter Macbeth and Soldiers.

Macbeth. Hang out our banners on the outward walls.

Women cry offstage as Seyton enters.

Macbeth. What is that noise?

Seyton. The Queen, my lord, is dead.

Macbeth. She should have died hereafter;
    There would have been time for such a word°.
    Tomorrow, and tomorrow, and tomorrow

Discovery: reconnaissance.   *There...word*: it would have been a better time for such a
message.

Macbeth. Creeps in this petty pace from day to day,
    To the last syllable of recorded time;
    And all our yesterdays have lighted fools
    The way to dusty death. Out, out, brief candle!
    Life's but a walking shadow, a poor player
    That struts and frets his hour upon the stage
    And then is heard no more. It is a tale
    Told by an idiot, full of sound and fury
    Signifying nothing.

Enter Messenger.

Macbeth. Thou com'st to use thy tongue; thy story quickly!

Messenger. Gracious my lord,
    I should report that which I say I saw,
    But know not how to do 't.

Macbeth.   Well, say, sir.

Messenger. As did I stand my watch upon the hill,
    I looked toward Birnam, and anon, methought,
    The wood began to move.

Macbeth.   Liar and slave!

Messenger. Let me endure your wrath, if 't be not so,
    Within this three mile may you see it coming;
    I say a moving grove.

Macbeth.   If thou speak'st false,
    Upon the next tree shalt thou hang alive,

Macbeth. Till famine cling° thee. "Fear not, till Birnam Wood
   Do come to Dunsinane!" And now a wood
   Comes toward Dunsinane. Arm, arm, and out!
   Ring the alarum bell! Blow wind, come wrack°!
   At least we'll die with harness on our back.

They exit.

Act V, Scene 6.
Dunsinane. Before the castle.

*Drums and colors. Enter Malcolm, Siward, Macduff, and their
army with boughs.*

Malcolm. Now near enough. Your leavy° screens throw down.
   You, worthy uncle, shall lead our first battle°.
   Worthy Macduff and we shall take upon
   What else remains to do, according to our order°.

Siward.   Fare you well.
   Do we° but find the tyrant's power° tonight,
   Let us be beaten, if we cannot fight.

Macduff. Make all our trumpets speak; give them all breath,
   Those clamorous harbingers of blood and death.

All exit. Alarums continue.

Cling: shrivel. *Wrack:* ruin. *Harness:* armor. *Leavy:* leafy. *Battle:* battalion.
Order: plan. *Do we:* if we do. *Power:* forces.

Act V, Scene 7.
Another part of the field.

Enter Macbeth.

Macbeth. They have tied me to a stake; I cannot fly,
But bearlike I must fight the course°. What's he
That was not born of woman? Such a one
Am I to fear or none.

Enter Young Siward.

Young Siward. What is thy name?

Macbeth.   Thou'lt be afraid to hear it.

Young Siward. No; though thou call'st thyself a hotter name
Than any is in hell.

Macbeth.   My name's Macbeth.

Young Siward. The devil himself could not pronounce a title
More hateful to mine ear.

Macbeth.   No, nor more fearful.

Young Siward. Thou liest, abhorrèd tyrant; with my sword
I'll prove the lie thou speak'st.

They fight and Young Siward is slain.

Course: round of bearbaiting.

Macbeth.   Thou wast born of woman.
   But swords I smile at, weapons laugh to scorn,
   Brandished by man that's of a woman born.

Macbeth carries Siward off. Alarums ring as Macduff enters.

Macduff. That way the noise is. Tyrant, show thy face!
   If thou be'st slain and with no stroke of mine,
   My wife and children' ghosts will haunt me still.
   Let me find him, Fortune! And more I beg not.

Macduff exits. Alarums ring as Malcolm and Siward enter.

Siward. This way, my lord. The castle's gently rend'red°.
   The tyrant's people on both sides do fight;
   The noble thanes do bravely in the war;
   The day almost itself professes° yours,
   And little is to do.

Malcolm. We have met with foes that strike beside us°.

Siward. Enter, sir, the castle.

The exit as alarums continue.

Act V, Scene 8.
Another part of the field.

Enter Macbeth.

Macbeth. Why should I play the Roman fool, and die

Rend'red: surrendered without a struggle.   *Itself professes*: declares itself.   *Strike beside us*: deliberately avoid striking us.

[Macbeth] On my own sword? Whiles I see lives°, the gashes
    Do better upon them. *[Enter Macduff]*

Macduff.   Turn, hell-hound, turn!

Macbeth. Of all men else I have avoided thee.
    But get thee back! My soul is too much charg'd
    With blood of thine already.

Macduff.   I have no words:
    My voice is in my sword, thou bloodier villain
    Than terms can give thee out°.

Macbeth. Let fall thy blade on vulnerable crests;
    I bear a charmèd life, which must not yield
    To one of woman born.

Macduff.   Despair thy charm,
    And let the angel°whom thou still hast served
    Tell thee, Macduff was from his mother's womb
    Untimely ripped.

Macbeth. Accursèd be that tongue that tells me so,
    For it hath cowed my better part of man°!
    I'll not fight with thee.

Macduff.   Then yield thee, coward,
    And live to be the show and gaze o' th' time°:
    Painted upon a pole°, and underwrit,
    "Here may you see the tyrant."

Whiles I see lives: as long as I see living men. *Terms...out*: words can describe you.
Angel: *i.e.* fallen angel or fiend. *Better part of man*: courage. *Gaze o' th' time*:
spectacle of the day. *Painted upon a pole*: *i.e.* displayed in a carnival.

Macbeth.   I will not yield.
    To kiss the ground before young Malcolm's feet,
    And to be baited with the rabble's curse.
    Though Birnam Wood be come to Dunsinane,
    And though opposed, being of no woman born,
    Yet I will try the last. Lay on, Macduff;
    And damned be him that first cries "Hold, enough!"

*They fight and Macbeth is slain. Exit Macduff with Macbeth's
body. Retreat and flourish. Drum and colors. Enter Malcolm,
Siward, Ross, Thanes, and Soldiers.*

Malcolm. I were the friends we miss were safe arrived

Siward. Some must go off°; and yet, by these I see,
    So great a day as this is cheaply bought.

Malcolm. Macduff is missing, and your noble son.

Ross. Your son, my lord, has paid a soldier's debt:
    He only lived but till he was a man;
    The which no sooner had his prowess confirmed
    In the unshrinking station° where he fought,
    But like a man he died.

Siward.   Then he is dead?

Ross. Ay, and brought off the field.

Siward.   Had he his hurts before?

Go off: die.   Unshrinking station: place where he held his ground.

Ross. Ay, on the front.

Siward.   Why then, G-d's soldier be he!
  And G-d be with him. Here comes newer comfort.

Enter Macduff with Macbeth's head.

Macduff. Hail, King! For so thou art: behold where stands
  Th' usurper's cursèd head. The time is free°.
  Hail, King of Scotland!

All.   Hail, King of Scotland!

Flourish.

Malcolm.   My thanes and kinsmen,
  Henceforth be earls, the first that ever Scotland
  In such an honor named. What's more to do,
  Which would be planted newly with the time°
  As calling home our exiled friends abroad
  That fled the snares of watchful tyranny,
  Producing forth the cruel ministers°
  Of this dead butcher and his fiendlike queen,
  Who, as 'tis thought, by self and violent° hands
  Took off her life; this, and what needful else
  That calls upon us°, by the grace of Grace
  We will perform in measure, time, and place°:
  So thanks to all at once and to each one
  Whom we invite to see us crowned at Scone.

Flourish as all exit.

The end.

Time is free: world is liberated. *Would...time:* will happen during this new era.
Ministers: representatives. *Violent:* her own violent. *Calls upon us:* requires my
attention. *In measure...place:* at the proper time and place.

Shakespeare: To Teach or Not to Teach

By Cass Foster and Lynn G. Johnson
The answer is a resounding "To Teach!"
There's nothing dull about this guide
for anyone teaching Shakespeare in the
classroom, with activities such as
crossword puzzles, a scavenger hunt,
warm-up games, and costume and
scenery suggestions.
ISBN 1-877749-03-6

The Sixty-Minute Shakespeare Series

By Cass Foster
Not enough time to tackle the
unabridged versions of the world's
most widely read playwright? Pick up a
copy of *Romeo and Juliet, A Midsummer
Night's Dream, Hamlet, Macbeth, Much
Ado About Nothing* and *Twelfth Night,*
and discover how much more accessi-
ble Shakespeare can be to you and
your students.

Letters of Love: Stories from the Heart

Edited by Salvatore Caputo
In this warm collection of love letters
and stories, a group of everyday people
shares hopes, dreams and experiences
of love: love won, love lost, and love
found again. Most of all, they share
their belief that love is a blessing that
makes life's challenges worthwhile.
ISBN 1-877749-35-4

Linda F. Radke's Promote Like a Pro: Small Budget, Big Show

By Linda F. Radke and contributors
In Linda F. Radke's *Promote Like a Pro:
Small Budget, Big Show,* a successful
publisher and a group of insiders offer
self-publishers a step-by-step guide on
how to use the print and broadcast
media, public relations, the Internet,
public speaking and other tools to mar-
ket books—without breaking the bank!
ISBN 1-877749-36-2

The Economical Guide to Self-Publishing

By Linda F. Radke
This book is a must-have for anyone
who is or wants to be a self-publisher.
It is a valuable step-by-step guide for
producing and promoting your book
effectively, even on a limited budget.
The book is filled with tips on avoiding
common, costly mistakes and provides
resources that can save you lots of
money—not to mention headaches. A
Writer's Digest Book Club selection.
ISBN 1-877749-16-8

That Hungarian's in My Kitchen

By Linda F. Radke
You won't want that Hungarian to leave
after you've tried some of the 125 Hun-
garian-American Kosher recipes that
fill this delightful cookbook. Written for
both the novice cook and the sophisti-
cated chef. It comes complete with
"Aunt Ethel's Helpful Hints."
ISBN 1-877749-28-1

Kosher Kettle: International Adventures in Jewish Cooking

*By Sybil Ruth Kaplan,
Foreword by Joan Nathan*
With more than 350 recipes from 27
countries, this is one Kosher cookbook
you don't want to be without. It
includes everything from wheat halva
from India to borrekas from Greece.
Five Star Publications is donating a
portion of all sales of *Kosher Kettle* to
MAZON: A Jewish Response to Hunger.
A *Jewish Book Club* selection.
ISBN 1-877749-19-2

Other Fine Titles From
Five Star Publications, Incorporated

Most titles are available through
www.BarnesandNoble.com and www.amazon.com

Household Careers: Nannies, Butlers, Maids & More: The Complete Guide for Finding Household Employment
By Linda F. Radke
There is a wealth of professional positions available in the child-care and home-help fields. This award-winning book provides all the information you need to find and secure a household job. ISBN 1-877749-05-2

Nannies, Maids & More: The Complete Guide for Hiring Household Help
By Linda F. Radke
Anyone who has had to hire household help knows what a nightmare it can be. This book provides a step-by-step guide to hiring—and keeping—household help, complete with sample ads, interview questions, and employment forms. ISBN 0-9619853-2-1

Profits of Death: An Insider Exposes the Death Care Industries
By Darryl J. Roberts
This book still has the funeral and cemetery industries reeling from aftershocks. Industry insider Darryl J. Roberts uncovers how the death care industry manipulates consumers into overspending at the most vulnerable time in their lives. He also tells readers everything they need to know about making final arrangements—including how to save up to 50% in costs. THIS IS ONE BOOK THEY CAN'T BURY! ISBN 1-877749-21-4

Shoah: Journey From the Ashes
By Cantor Leo Fettman
and Paul M. Howey
Cantor Leo Fettman survived the horrors of Auschwitz while millions of others, including almost his entire family, did not. He worked in the crematorium, was experimented on by Dr. Josef Mengele, and lived through an attempted hanging by the SS. His remarkable tale of survival and subsequent joy is an inspiration for all. *Shoah* includes a historical prologue that chronicles the 2,000 years of anti-Semitism that led to the Holocaust. Cantor Fettman's message is one of love and hope, yet it contains an important warning to new generations to remember—in order to avoid repeating—the evils of the past.
ISBN 0-9679721-0-8

For the Record: A Personal Facts and Document Organizer
By Ricki Sue Pagano
Many people have trouble keeping track of the important documents and details of their lives. Ricki Sue Pagano designed *For the Record* so they could regain control—and peace of mind. This organizing tool helps people keep track and makes it easy to find important documents in a pinch.
ISBN 0-9670226-0-6

Tying the Knot: The Sharp Dresser's Guide to Ties and Handkerchiefs
By Andrew G. Cochran
This handy little guide contains everything you want (or need) to know about neckties, bow ties, pocket squares, and handkerchiefs—from coordinating ties and shirts to tying a variety of knots.
ISBN 0-9630152-6-5

Other Fine Titles From
Five Star Publications, Incorporated

Most titles are available through
www.BarnesandNoble.com and www.amazon.com

Phil Rea's How to Become a Millionaire Selling Remodeling
By Phil Rea
All successful remodelers know how to use tools. Too few, however, know how to use the tools of selling. Phil Rea mastered the art of selling remodeling and made more than $1,000,000 at his craft. He has shared his secrets through coast-to-coast seminars. Now, for the first time, you can read how to make the most of the financial opportunities remodeling has to offer.
ISBN 1-877749-29-x

Joe Boyd's Build It Twice...If You Want a Successful Building Project
By Joe Boyd
In *Joe Boyd's Build It Twice...If You Want a Successful Building Project*, construction expert Joe Boyd shares his 40 years of experience with construction disputes and explains why they arise. He also outlines a strategy that will allow project owners to avoid most construction woes: Build the project on paper first!
ISBN 0-9663620-0-4

Light in the Darkness
By St. George T. Lee
Physician St. George T. Lee's sex addiction cost him his career and nearly his family. In *Light in the Darkness*, Dr. Lee talks openly of his treatment and how he fought to regain the respect of his family. His book will serve as a beacon of inspiration for others affected by addictive behaviors of any kind.
ISBN 0-967891-0-1

Getting Your Shift Together: Making Sense of Organizational Culture *and Change*
By P.J. Bouchard and Lizz Pellett
Few things are inevitable: death, taxes—and change. In today's fast-paced business environment, changes come in staggering succession, yet few corporate change initiatives succeed. *Getting Your Shift Together: Making Sense of Organizational Culture* and Change offers solutions to make change an ally that boosts morale, productivity, and the bottom line.
ISBN 0-9673248-0-7

Keys to the Asylum
By Dr. Daniel K. Bloomfield
Invited to become the dean of a one-year medical school in Urbana-Champaign, Dr. Daniel K. Bloomfield said he would have to decline the offer if there were no plans to make it a full four-year school. "Well, that might happen," the bureaucrats said. On that thin hope, he became enmeshed in a 14-year battle with the system: first, to create an innovative medical curriculum on a low budget, then to expand the school, and then to simply keep it alive. Dr. Bloomfield has recorded his grueling experience in *Keys to the Asylum: a Dean, a Medical School, and Academic Politics.* ISBN 0-9701022-0-8

The Proper Pig's Guide to Mealtime Manners
By L.A. Kowal and Sally Starbuck Stamp
Of course, no one in your family would ever be a pig at mealtime, but perhaps you know another family with that problem. This whimsical guide, complete with its own ceramic pig, gives valuable advice for children and adults alike on how to make mealtimes more fun and mannerly.
ISBN 1-877749-20-6

DATE DUE
